19.95

THE RAINBOW ROCKET

To my friends and family,
and to the tea, the walk, and the paintbrush.
— *Kristi Bridgeman*

Dedicated to my son and my mother,
and to all children who have faced the
loss of someone very dear to them.
— *Fiona Tinwei Lam*

Acknowledgements: The author gratefully acknowledges Barbara Nickel, Stephanie Maricevic, Loretta Seto, Susan Olding, Jane Hamilton Silcott, Judy MacFarlane, Don Sedgwick and Shona and Bruce Lam for their encouragement, advice and support, with special thanks to her son, Robbie Lam-Tolliday and her mother, Dr. Bik May Wai Lam for their inspiration and love.

The author is donating her share of the proceeds from the sale of this book to the Alzheimer's Society of B.C.

We gratefully acknowledge the financial support of the Canada Council for the Arts, the British Columbia Arts Council through the BC Ministry of Tourism, Culture, and the Arts, and the Government of Canada through the Canada Book Fund, for our publishing activities.

Published by Oolichan Books
P.O. Box 2278, Fernie, B.C. V0B 1M0 Canada

www.oolichan.com
Printed in Canada

Library and Archives Canada Cataloguing in Publication

Lam, Fiona Tinwei, 1964–
    The rainbow rocket / Fiona Tinwei Lam ;
    Kristi Bridgeman, illustrator.

ISBN 978-0-88982-288-7

I. Bridgeman, Kristi, 1961– II. Title.

PS8573.A38383R35 2013   jC813'.6   C2012-908015-2

THE RAINBOW ROCKET

By

Fiona Tinwei Lam

Illustrated by

Kristi Bridgeman

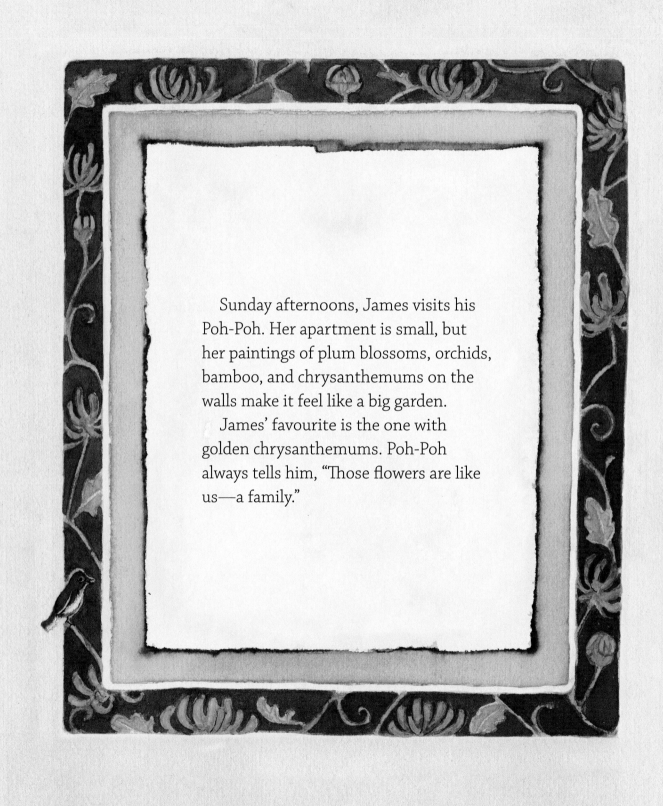

Sunday afternoons, James visits his Poh-Poh. Her apartment is small, but her paintings of plum blossoms, orchids, bamboo, and chrysanthemums on the walls make it feel like a big garden.

James' favourite is the one with golden chrysanthemums. Poh-Poh always tells him, "Those flowers are like us—a family."

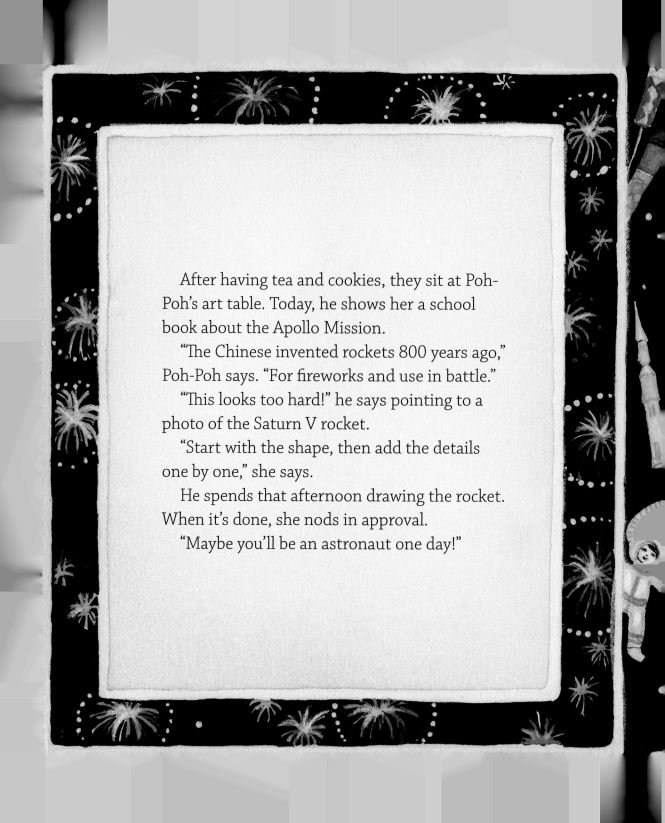

After having tea and cookies, they sit at Poh-Poh's art table. Today, he shows her a school book about the Apollo Mission.

"The Chinese invented rockets 800 years ago," Poh-Poh says. "For fireworks and use in battle."

"This looks too hard!" he says pointing to a photo of the Saturn V rocket.

"Start with the shape, then add the details one by one," she says.

He spends that afternoon drawing the rocket. When it's done, she nods in approval.

"Maybe you'll be an astronaut one day!"

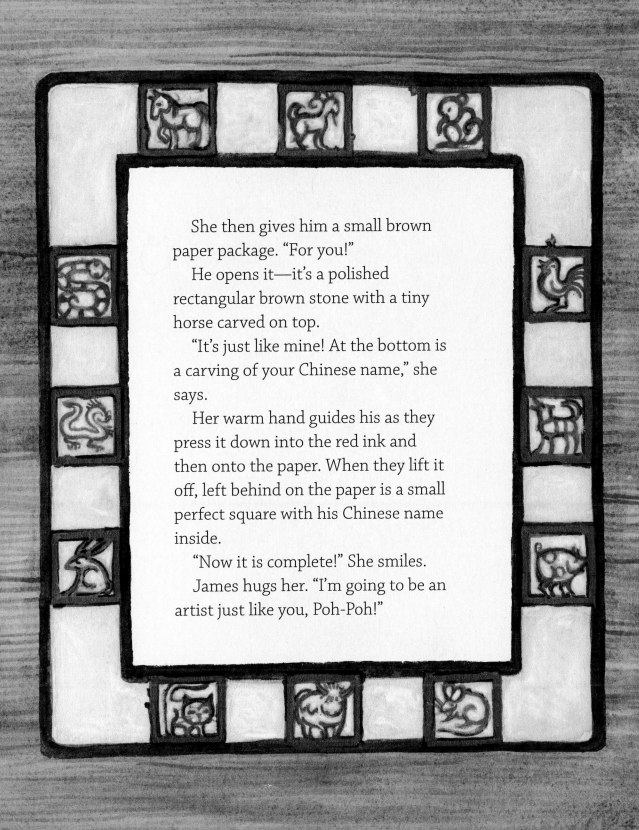

She then gives him a small brown paper package. "For you!"

He opens it—it's a polished rectangular brown stone with a tiny horse carved on top.

"It's just like mine! At the bottom is a carving of your Chinese name," she says.

Her warm hand guides his as they press it down into the red ink and then onto the paper. When they lift it off, left behind on the paper is a small perfect square with his Chinese name inside.

"Now it is complete!" She smiles.

James hugs her. "I'm going to be an artist just like you, Poh-Poh!"

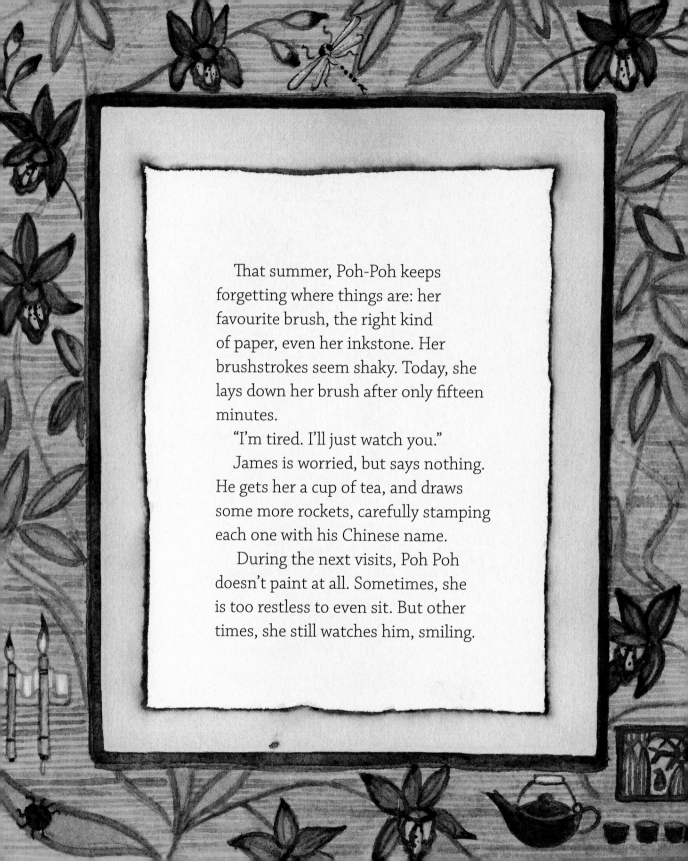

That summer, Poh-Poh keeps forgetting where things are: her favourite brush, the right kind of paper, even her inkstone. Her brushstrokes seem shaky. Today, she lays down her brush after only fifteen minutes.

"I'm tired. I'll just watch you."

James is worried, but says nothing. He gets her a cup of tea, and draws some more rockets, carefully stamping each one with his Chinese name.

During the next visits, Poh Poh doesn't paint at all. Sometimes, she is too restless to even sit. But other times, she still watches him, smiling.

"Hi, hi, hi!" Poh-Poh says, clapping her hands when she sees James and his mom arrive at her new nursing home the following autumn.

He runs over to hug her. It stops raining so they go outside for a walk. James tries to talk to her, but he's not sure now how much Poh-Poh understands. Frustrated, he goes silent.

Suddenly Poh-Poh stops. A sunbeam from a break in the clouds makes her face glow. She points toward the sky. He looks up.

"A rainbow, Poh-Poh!" he shouts.
Ribbons of colour arc over the city. Everything
sparkles! Only when the rainbow fades do they
head back inside.

One day, during their walk, Poh-Poh doesn't look at anything, not even the red leaves on the maples. As they step off the curb, she almost loses her balance. James and his mom hold her arms to keep her steady.

"Home, home!" she says suddenly.

Poh-Poh holds his hand too tightly, but he doesn't complain.

When they reach her room, James takes out one of his rocket drawings from his knapsack. He points out the rainbow he's added. "Poh-Poh, remember?"

As his mother puts his picture on the window, he sighs. "I miss our Sunday afternoons," he says softly.

His grandmother shuffles up to his drawing and gently traces his rainbow with her fingers, and then his name.

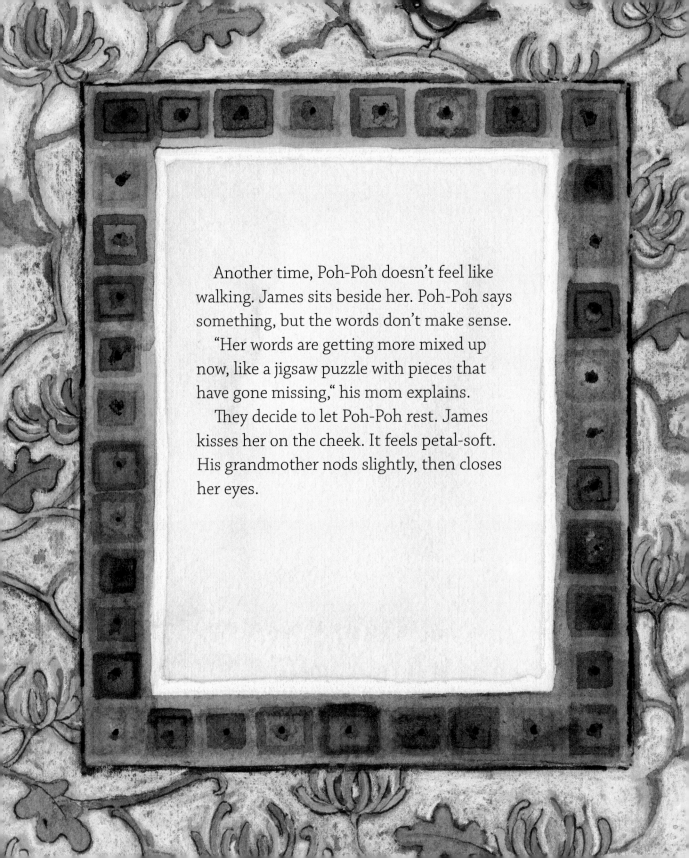

Another time, Poh-Poh doesn't feel like walking. James sits beside her. Poh-Poh says something, but the words don't make sense.

"Her words are getting more mixed up now, like a jigsaw puzzle with pieces that have gone missing," his mom explains.

They decide to let Poh-Poh rest. James kisses her on the cheek. It feels petal-soft. His grandmother nods slightly, then closes her eyes.

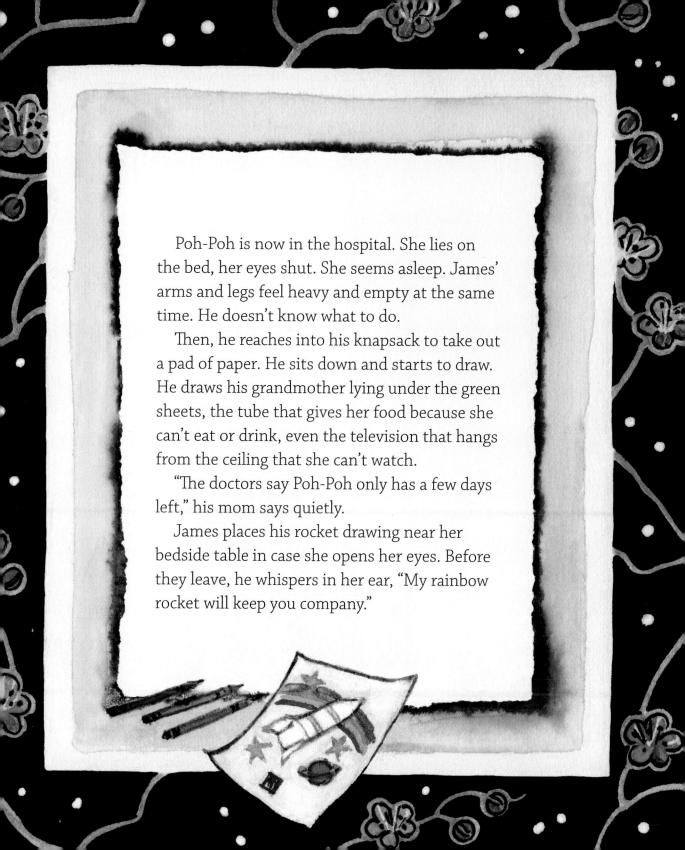

Poh-Poh is now in the hospital. She lies on the bed, her eyes shut. She seems asleep. James' arms and legs feel heavy and empty at the same time. He doesn't know what to do.

Then, he reaches into his knapsack to take out a pad of paper. He sits down and starts to draw. He draws his grandmother lying under the green sheets, the tube that gives her food because she can't eat or drink, even the television that hangs from the ceiling that she can't watch.

"The doctors say Poh-Poh only has a few days left," his mom says quietly.

James places his rocket drawing near her bedside table in case she opens her eyes. Before they leave, he whispers in her ear, "My rainbow rocket will keep you company."

That night James dreams that he is inside his
own rocket ship. Planets and stars whiz past.

Soon, the ship lands.
The hatch opens. He's in the middle of a
huge garden with flowers as tall as people.

He follows a path to a small clearing. Poh-Poh is there, painting at a table surrounded by paper scrolls. She smiles up at him as though she's been expecting him. "Come and see!"

Her words have come back! Relieved, he runs to hug her, then looks at her painting. It's a horse, just like the one on the stamp she gave him.

Before his eyes, it emerges from the page, grows and grows—into a real horse, shaking its mane and tail!

"Go for a ride!" Poh-Poh urges.

He climbs on. The horse leaps up and soars over the garden.

When they return, Poh-Poh has painted him a bowl of luscious peaches. He touches them— they become real too! They sit on the grass to eat. When he's full, he starts yawning, and soon falls asleep in his grandmother's arms.

"A butterfly leaves behind its chrysalis. Poh-Poh's spirit, what made her alive, left her body in the same way," his mom says after Poh-Poh dies.

When James walks past the bare trees on his way to school, he thinks of how her brushstrokes made flowers, leaves and birds appear on paper like magic. When he draws, he tries imagining that he's back with Poh-Poh. But it isn't enough.

"I miss her so much," he tells his mom.

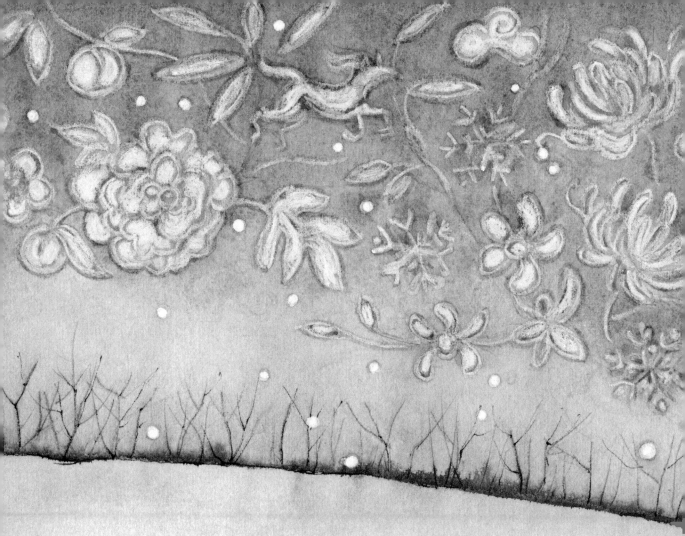

When she reminds him about Ching Ming Day
coming up, he remembers how families bring food to the
cemetery and burn incense and paper money, and even
sometimes paper clothes or other things made out of
paper as gifts to send to their loved ones who have died.
His mother has told him that it's a way to show that the
family still cares.

James thinks about what Poh Poh would have liked.
"Can we bring other things too?" he asks.

"Why not?" his mom says.

On Ching Ming day, many families gather at the cemetery. Flowers, incense sticks, fruit, and tiny cups of wine decorate the graves. Some families have brought food. Others are burning paper money as offerings to their ancestors. A few small children are playing around a tree.

After they sweep the grave, James helps his mom set out some flowers and oranges. To show respect, they bow in front of the grave three times.

Out of his knapsack, James takes out the new rainbow rocket drawing that he's made especially for today, just like the one in his dream. He's even drawn a bowl of peaches inside.